Utzing

Schongau Festing Staffel-See

Mönchaltorf hoch. Süd-Dorf

Dimitring

Westbahnhof

Waalhausen Kaltenbrg Erding Fildstng

Oberstall Türkenfeld Gültendorf Grafrath

Lech Kindach Inning Stegen

Iglsing Schondorf Liedwau

Mosbach Friedberg Diessen

Sitzau Greifenberg Elfriede See Eching

Schliße +125 +328 Utting

Landsberg am Lech Herrsching

Landsberg West Landsberg Hbf Herrsching Bf.

Scheifling Kaufering Andechs

Vilgertshofen Leichling

Stadt Pützenberg

Jesing Hohenpeißenberg

Stoffen Ummendorf Hbf.

Plürgen Ummendorf

Winglings See Ummendorf-City

Fluck + zighofen Winglingdorf Ummendorf Süd Bf.

mühlhausen

genheim

Osthetten Roth

Thaining

Königliche Eisenbahn Ummendorf – Prag
Králowská Železnice Ummendorf–Praha
Maßstab 1 : 300 000
Ummendorf Anno 1905

To our dear Patrick with love! Grandma Dori & Grandpa Joe

Copyright © 1987 Nord-Süd Verlag, Mönchaltorf, Switzerland
First published in Switzerland under the title Piro und die Dampflok
English text copyright © 1987 Rosemary Lanning
Copyright English language edition under the imprint
North-South Books © 1987 Rada Matija AG, Staefa, Switzerland

First published in Great Britain, Canada, Australia
and New Zealand in 1987 by North-South Books, an imprint
of Rada Matija AG.

Distributed in Great Britain by
Blackie and Son Ltd, 7 Leicester Place,
London WC2H 7BP.
British Library Cataloguing in Publication Data

Baumann, Kurt
  Piro and the runaway train.
  I. Title II. Bernard, Jiří III. Piro
  und die Dampflok. *English*
  833'.914[J] PZ7

ISBN 0-200-72901-2

Distributed in Canada by
Douglas & McIntyre Ltd., Toronto.
Canadian Cataloguing in Publication Data available in
Marc Record from National Library of Canada.
ISBN 0 88894 786 0

Distributed in Australia and New Zealand by
Buttercup Books Pty. Ltd., Melbourne.
ISBN 0 949447 36 6

Printed in Germany

PIRO
and the Runaway Train

By Kurt Baumann
Translated by Rosemary Lanning
With pictures by Jiří Bernard

North-South Books
London   Toronto   Melbourne

Behind the house where Piro and his Aunt Emily lived was a railway siding. It belonged to an old station whose broken window panes seemed to blink sleepily in the sun. Sometimes a train still thundered past, and Piro watched it wistfully, but it was many years since any trains had actually stopped at the little station.

The tracks of the siding were completely rusted and between the sleepers grew tufts of tall grass. But the thing that interested Piro most was a small, abandoned engine standing next to the buffers. It looked wonderful. All right, the chimney was rusted and the paint was flaking off, but the rivets were still holding fast and perhaps everything could be put back in working order.

When Piro asked his Aunt for money she said, "Whatever do you want with that ugly old thing?" But she gave him the money all the same. Piro bought some paint and a hammer. He hammered away at the engine until all the old paint had fallen off. Then he painted everything afresh. He used green paint so that the engine wouldn't show up so much against its surroundings. Then he took the ladder away and stepped back a few paces. Now the engine looked super! Really great! And with so much green all around it you'd hardly know it was there.

Piro didn't know much about steam trains. He had once heard that this sort of engine was called a Little Tiger and the teacher at school had explained how a steam engine works. All Piro remembered was that steam flowed through something and some rods went backwards and forwards to make the wheels move. But the most important thing was that steam comes from boiling water, and for that you need fire.

In Aunt Emily's cellar was a central heating boiler and right next to it was a heap of coal. Piro filled some buckets with coal, carried them to his engine and emptied them into the bunker. Then he dragged out the garden hose and filled the water tanks. Now all he had to do was light the fire. That was easy. He fetched matches from the kitchen, and some old newspapers and kindling wood. Then he opened the fire door, lit the fire and added coal to it. Soon smoke was rising from the chimney. Piro felt very proud of himself.

Pirate, Piro's dog, trotted along the track looking rather anxious. Piro called him and lifted him onto the footplate. Then he climbed up there himself, stood in front of all the gauges, wheels and levers and looked through the oval windows. He reached down a train driver's old cap from a hook and put it on, then shovelled a bit more coal into the fire so that the engine wouldn't run out of steam.

"All clear ahead!" cried Piro, excitedly. Now Little Tiger was waking up from its long sleep. It began to make a drumming noise and started to move. At first it went quite slowly, then faster and faster. Piro was startled. He didn't know where the brakes were. He pulled a lever, but that only produced a shrill "peep!". It was the whistle! Pirate stood up, nervously. Piro stroked him and looked through the window. The track stretched away into the distance and out of sight.

Piro was beginning to enjoy clattering through the countryside. He shovelled more coal on the fire and stopped worrying about the brakes.

A few moments later another track appeared beside theirs, then another. Ahead the two tracks crossed one another. "How will we get through that?" wondered Piro, but everything was all right. With a few rumbles the engine rode over the points, and Piro sighed with relief. Suddenly he caught sight of a signal. Luckily it was up, so the line was clear. On one side a signal box flashed by. A man with a red peaked cap watched them go past, shaking his head. Piro felt guilty, but what could he do? Suddenly the tracks untangled themselves and Little Tiger steamed onwards. Church towers and neat villages came into sight with a rattle and then were gone.

Piro shovelled the last of his coal into the fire box. But then more tracks appeared, and more and more. There was a signal ahead. It was down! The little engine carried on regardless. Then, as if by magic, the signal was raised.

More and more tracks, more and more signals came into sight. "We must be close to a big station," thought Piro. Their speed was dropping now. The engine was running out of steam. "I just hope we can stop before we run into the station!" thought Piro. But the engine wasn't slowing down quickly enough. "I must let off some steam," thought Piro. "Then we will lose power." He pulled the lever for the whistle.

The whistle sounded again and again and steam hissed into the air. The drumming gradually stopped, but the engine was still clattering along. Gradually it slowed down, and as they came into the station, the

engine was rolling along very gently. Then there was a slight jolt and Little Tiger stopped at the buffers.

In the station a few people looked at them curiously, but Piro just tucked his dog under his arm and disappeared into the crowd. He felt hungry now and of course Pirate needed something to eat and drink as well. Piro found the station buffet and went inside.

The only empty seats were at a table in one corner. A man in uniform was sitting there and beside him was an engine driver's cap exactly like Piro's! Piro sat down next to him and ordered a bowl of water for his dog, a sausage and some bread. He cut the sausage in two and gave one half to Pirate who gulped it down and wagged his tail. "Now, where did you pop up from?" asked the engine driver, looking at Piro's cap. Piro told him all about his journey. The engine driver raised his eyebrows at first. Then he began to laugh, clapped Piro on the shoulder, called the waiter and ordered Piro and Pirate another sausage. "Well, as you didn't find the brakes you did exactly the right thing. You let off steam." Piro felt proud. "But it was very dangerous just to drive off like that, you know. Have you any idea how many trains and people you put in danger?"

Piro said, "But all the signals were raised. The line was clear."

"That was just as well for you. Could you have stopped if the signals had been down?"

"No," said Piro quietly.

"Indeed. And why were they all raised, do you think?" asked the engine driver.

"I suppose I was lucky," guessed Piro.

"Not at all," said the engine driver. "They watched the control panel in the signal box to see where you were and diverted the other trains or forced them to wait until you had gone past. That was the only way they could prevent an accident." Piro gulped and looked ashamed. But the train driver patted him on the head. "Come along," he said. "I'll show you my engine. It's five o'clock and I have to clock in."

The engine driver led Piro to a splendid red and blue streamlined train. They climbed into the cab and Piro gazed at all the dials and indicators on the instrument panel. The engine driver flicked a few switches and turned a big wheel and the train started to glide silently along. "This is a French high-speed train, a TGV. It's the fastest in Europe. It goes at 250 kilometres per hour, but could just as easily do 350," explained the driver. Piro was amazed. You could hardly tell that the train was moving and yet it was already travelling faster than his steam engine. Then it braked silently, stopped, started once more and pulled into the station again. "How exciting!" thought Piro. And yet something was missing...

Piro took the engine driver to see his Little Tiger. It was standing all alone, not a wisp of smoke rising from its chimney, but suddenly two men appeared, wearing red caps trimmed with gold braid. "This engine must stay here," said one of them sternly.

"Was it you who stole it?" asked the other man. The engine driver put his arm round Piro and told them his story. "So you see," he said at the end, "the boy was clever enough to let off steam when he couldn't find the brakes." The two officials looked a little less stern.

"Can I drive the engine back home?" asked Piro quickly.

"No, you can't do that," said the men. "It's much too dangerous."

"Well, I could drive it," said the engine driver. "There's another four hours until my train has to leave. I'll be back long before then."

"What will you do for coal?"

"I'll get hold of some." The officials nodded and went away.

The engine driver went to the phone and ordered some coal. A truck came and Piro and the engine driver took turns shovelling coal into the bunker. Piro lit the fire and Little Tiger began to move. Steam streamed back over the engine again and Little Tiger rattled steadily along. Church towers came into sight and now and then a signal, sometimes down. "This is the brake valve, this the brake pressure gauge, and this thing here is the emergency brake. But we don't need that at the moment," explained the engine driver, turning various wheels. The engine came to a slow halt in front of the signal. Then the journey continued. "You see, the fire heats the boiler and the steam flows through here and is re-heated. Then it forces its way into the cylinder where the two pistons pump backwards and forwards. The pistons are attached to piston rods which turn the wheels." Piro didn't quite follow all of that, but he felt safe because the engine driver seemed to understand it all.

They turned into the siding next to Aunt Emily's house and the engine driver brought Little Tiger to a halt just in front of the buffers. They said goodbye and Piro thanked the engine driver. He watched him walk all the way up the hill to the bus stop. The driver stopped once and looked back, smiling and waving his cap. Piro raised his own cap and waved back.

When Piro got home, his Aunt was rather cross. "Where have you
been all this time?" she shouted. "That engine was gone, too, the one
you wasted good money on, buying paint."
"It's back now," said Piro, proudly laying his engine driver's cap next
to his plate, from which rose a delicious smell of hot soup.

Jizerské hory
Orlické hory
Johanngeorgenstadt
Frýdland
Josefův Důl
Celnice
Grünten
Zollhaus
Burgberg
Dejvice
Vinohrady
Střelecký Ostrov
Praha
Vyšehrad
Braník
Podolí
Smíchov
Zbraslav
Mokropsy
Bílá Hora
Lomnický Štít
Slovenský Ráj
Vysoký Újezd
Karlštejn
Pitzling
Göring
Elligkofen
Budějovice
Klatovy
Blatná
Vltava
Rožmberk
Český Krumlov
Vysoké Tatry
Nízké Tatry